VICTORY II

A LEGACY ANTHOLOGY IN MEMORY OF
VE DAY - MAY 8TH 1945

Written by the
ELECTRIC ECLECTIC AUTHORS & FRIENDS

Electric EE Eclectic

VICTORY IN EUROPE

VICTORY IN EUROPE

Edition one (*Published as Victory-75*)
Copyright © 2020
Revised edition (*Published as Victory in Europe*)
Copyright © 2025

ALL RIGHTS RESERVED. No part of this publication may be reproduced, distributed, or transmitted in any form or by any means, including photocopying, recording, or other electronic or mechanical methods, or for digitally controlled lending, without the prior written permission of the publisher, except in the case of brief quotations embodied in critical reviews and certain other non-commercial uses permitted by copyright law.

Electric Eclectic Books/TOAD Publishing

Toadpublishing@mail.com

VICTORY IN EUROPE

The Human Author of this book states it excludes AI-generated content

VICTORY IN EUROPE

Introduction

When Coronavirus struck the world in 2020, the British VE Day celebrations, acknowledging 75 years since VE Day, could not proceed as planned.
The original version of this book was published to coincide with those celebrations.

The 80th anniversary of this momentous occasion is recognised this year, 2025. It may well be the last occasion for 'those who were there', those who experienced the celebrations to pay their respects.

Our Electric Eclectic Authors came together with friends to help celebrate the day the war ended in Europe with a series of short stories.
Each of these stories share a common, captivating theme, they are dedicated to the brave, often unsung heroes, the soldiers, nurses, and 'ordinary' civilians who fought tirelessly for our freedoms and liberties, on and off the battlefields, at home, or abroad.

In the rear of this book is list of contributing authors, and where you can find more of their work.

We would appreciate it if you could find a few moments to leave a review on the bookstore site from which made this purchase.
Thank you

VICTORY IN EUROPE

VICTORY IN EUROPE

TABLE OF CONTENTS

The Dome of St Paul's - *Karen J Mossman*

Patricia, Annie, and Jean - *Paul White*

Butterflies of Dunkirk - *Claire Plaisted*

Rosemary for Remembrance - *Julia Blake*

We'll Meet Again - *Jane Risdon*

99th Squadron - *Audrina Lane*

About The Electric Eclectic Books

VICTORY IN EUROPE

VICTORY IN EUROPE

The Dome of St. Paul's

BY KAREN J MOSSMAN

From my flat window, I can make out the majestic dome of St. Paul's Cathedral in the distance, its stonework gleaming faintly in the sunlight. Whenever I spot it, I know this is where I belong. All my life, it has been an iconic symbol.

Grandad Jack, my namesake, adored that place; the memories of him there are still vivid. As a treat, he would take me to the whispering gallery; I loved sitting there, listening to our voices echo and swirl around the dome, returning to us in a soft murmur.

VICTORY IN EUROPE

"It's a great place to reflect, lad," he'd say, "and just to listen. God gave us ears for a reason. We should use them."

That's what I did, and it probably saved my life in the Falklands. If I'd not heard that missile heading our way. I wouldn't be here now.

Back in the present, the television played quietly in the corner. It showed preparations for the VE day celebrations. Seventy-five years had passed since Churchill announced Germany had surrendered.

My grandparents told me stories about the war years. We sat in their cosy lounge on Redmond Street with a fire burning in the grate.
"We couldn't believe what we were hearing when we gathered around the radio. It felt like it would never end." Gran said with a sigh. "It was 1945, and we'd lived through some terrible times."

VICTORY IN EUROPE

My grandparents shaped my life. It wasn't until I grew up that I realised what people wonderful people they were.

"As long as I can see the dome of St. Pauls, I know I'm home." Grandad often said, and I took that to heart.
From my fifteenth-floor flat in the tower block, I could see the sprawling London skyline, a breathtaking panorama of buildings. When I spot them, it gives me a sense of home.

Today is the parade to commemorate the end of the war. Hundreds of people will come together to remember what happened that day. It's personal because I lived through it with my grandparent's stories.
Those brave soldiers found it difficult to talk about their experiences. Many had gone through terrible traumas. Men in those days suffered without the help they receive today because PTSD wasn't a recognised disorder.

VICTORY IN EUROPE

The television presenter talked about the preparations for the parade, and how the Queen would meet soldiers who played key parts in the war efforts.

Once more, the memory transported me back to the dimly lit lounge on Redmond Street, the scent of Gran's baking heavy in the air. Grandad sat by the fire smoking a pipe.
Gran was at the sink washing dishes in the sink when she told this story. I can see her now, her back to me as her hands busy in the water, her head slightly raised as she stared out of the window.

"We went to Buckingham Palace, dressed in red, white, and blue, the colours of our flag. Thousands of people made their way into the centre of London. There was music, singing, and dancing. It was wonderful. When we reached the gates, the King and Queen came onto the balcony with the little princesses and waved." Gran paused, turned to us, as her eyes rested on me.

VICTORY IN EUROPE

"It was a magical time, Jack. We were so used to searchlights and bombers streaking across the sky, so to see fireworks instead was such a thrill. Some people even built bonfires and burned effigies of Hitler."

As a young boy, my imagination picked up on everything and it felt like I experienced it with her.

"To think that our queen was one of those princesses on the balcony that day is incredible."
The stories were still vivid in my memory. Little boys are like sponges and absorb whatever they're told. I re-enacted battles with my toy military men.

Horses charged across my battlefields, and cannons exploded. Everything became real in my childish mind. I saw it all. I even had a bowl on a box to represent the dome of St. Paul's for when the soldiers returned home.

VICTORY IN EUROPE

Keeping my eyes on the clock, I moved around my flat as I waited for Emily, my granddaughter, to arrive. Thoughts of my grandparents continued to fill my head.

"Come here, lad." Grandad patted the chair next to him at the table one day.

I knew he wanted to tell me about a battle, so I brought the tin containing my soldiers.

"Before you empty them out, get a tablecloth," he instructed.

Gran rose to her feet and opened the sideboard drawer and handed me a dark blue one. I handed it to him and watched him cover the table with it.

"This is the sea," he said. "You'll need your boats out for this tale."

I ran into the front room and returned with several toys, eager to know what we were going to do.

With the cloth now on the table, Grandad set up the soldiers. "I was in the British Eighth Army, and the boat took us and dropped off in Salerno. Have you heard of it?"

VICTORY IN EUROPE

"No," I replied, gazing at him earnestly.
"It's in a place in Scilly. The Canadians and Americans were already fighting the Germans on the beaches, so they put our regiment off in the sea under the cover of darkness. But the canny buggers knew we were there and took pot shots. We were defenceless, standing waist deep, trying to get ashore and dodging bullets at the same time."
"Couldn't you climb back on the boats?" I asked.
"They'd gone. Soon as they dropped us off in the shallows, they returned to base. We felt abandoned to our fate. Many good men died. I thought I would too, but somehow made it onto the beach.

"Eventually, we gained control of the area and helped the Americans fight the Germans, and the battle raged for hours. We won that one, but it was at a high cost."

He looked over at Gran, who watched us quietly.
"They shouldn't have abandoned us like that."

VICTORY IN EUROPE

All the time Grandad spoke, he shifted the toy men and the boats around the table. His fingers taking pot shots, as he flicked them backwards with his finger as they died. It was something I'll never forget.

"We were supposed to return to base for a rest, but news came in of a Canadian regiment surrounded by German tanks. We couldn't leave them. After leapfrogging through and dodging bullets, we went in with guns blazing.

With a lot of effort, we blasted a hole in the armoured vehicles. The Germans fled." His eyes glinted with amusement at the memory.

The Canadian government awarded Grandad's battalion the Maple Leaf battle honour. I own it now and one day it will belong to my granddaughter, Emily.

"We wore it on our uniforms with pride." Absently, he placed his hand on where the badge would have been.

VICTORY IN EUROPE

"Battles fought and battles won," He would say that like a chant. I knew he thought about his friend who never made it back.

Later, Grandad and a group from his regiment were in the Po Valley in Italy when renegade Germans captured them. Later, they abandoned their prisoners, and instead of killing them, took their boots, leaving the men bare-footed. Grandad and his comrades walked many miles until they came to a Canadian camp.

Soldiers aimed guns at them, and they entered with their arms raised. When their military spotted the Maple Leaf honour sewn onto their British uniforms, they welcomed in and adorned with cigarettes and chocolates.

No one ever talks about the great distances covered on foot during the wartime period, but Emily did. She did a lot of research regarding where they marched. She wrote it on her blog internet thing explaining how

VICTORY IN EUROPE

people covered hundreds of miles across vast countries.

The doorbell rang, returning my focus to the present. Emily had arrived.

She enjoyed the war stories I passed down, and it inspired her to join up. Just like her great grandfather, she travelled the world. Unlike him, she didn't have to see it on foot.

Emily looked smart in her uniform and greeted me with a warm smile and a kiss. "You look lovely, Grandad," she said, referring to my uniform and display of medals. "As do you, Em. Are you ready to do this?"

"I am," she said. "I'll be proud to walk beside you."

We made our way to Trafalgar Square, along with crowds of other people. It made me think again of Gran and her tales of VE Day. It was even possible that she walked the same streets, not knowing whether her husband would return safely.

VICTORY IN EUROPE

Grandad was one of the lucky ones. So many didn't come home. So many men died in the war, leaving behind grieving families who never knew where their loved ones were buried. Their last resting places lost to the chaos of battle.

"All these folks, Grandad," Emily said with surprise in her voice. "Just imagine if they all died. That's how many perished in the Great Grandad's war."

"And more, love." My eyes swept around the men and women who walked in our direction.

The estimate is that 75 million individuals lost their lives worldwide. That's a hard figure to grasp. It's more than all the people who live in English and Wales today. Too copious to apprehend.

We joined our place in the parade with others in uniforms and slowly began moving forward towards the Square.

"In June 2022, do you think they will do this to commemorate your war?" My granddaughter asked.

VICTORY IN EUROPE

My war. She always referred to the Falklands as mine, as opposed to her two tours in Afghanistan.

"If I'm still alive," I laughed.

She playfully punched my arm. "You're not going anywhere."

We took our place as Queen Elizabeth arrived with the Duke of Edinburgh and greeted people at the other end of the line to where we were.

Emily gave me a big smile. "You make me very proud, Grandad," she said again.

"I am proud of you too, love. My grandparents would have loved you and all you've done."

Her eyes shone, and the corners of her mouth twitched.

The queen approached us, and I straightened the edge of my trousers, making sure they were neatly tucked under my knee.

"Hello." Her Majesty said, as she held out her gloved hand for me to shake. She glanced at the medals and

ribbons hanging proudly on my chest. "Isn't it lovely that so many people are here?"
I nodded, almost overcome by seeing her close up. "My Gran came to see you at the Palace on VE Day. She was one of the thousands at the gate waving."

Queen Elizabeth smiled. "I remember that day well. I think we all do, well, those of us who are left."
Her Majesty then stepped towards Emily, who curtsied and placed a hand on my shoulder. "This is my Grandad Jack. He was on the HMS Coventry in the Falklands war. If he hadn't heard the missile coming over, he would have died, too."

The Monarch glanced back at me. "Without brave people like you and your families, we probably wouldn't be here today."
o my granddaughter, she said, "It's a pleasant afternoon. I am so pleased you could come." She moved on to greet the next person in line.
We ended the day wandering around St Paul's Cathedral.

VICTORY IN EUROPE

My thoughts returned once more to my grandad, grateful that he spoke about his past.
Emily and I, along with so many others, could make sure it was never forgotten.

Dedicated to my grandfather, Cyril Parry of Chester, whose war history I've included here

VICTORY IN EUROPE

VICTORY IN EUROPE

VICTORY IN EUROPE

PATRICIA, ANNIE AND JEAN

BY PAUL WHITE

I have written this story as a monologue, blending many historical facts with fictional instances to create a gentle but emotional account of wartime life from a young woman's perspective.

It's hard for me to believe VE Day was so long ago when, within a moment, I can recall those times as if they were yesterday; even the scents prevail, preserved within my memory, waiting to be stirred into life once again as my thoughts flit back and forth. The incredible release from fear and pain that, at last, encompassed us can only be described by those who experienced it.

I think the words 'flit back and forth' are the most reasonable way I can describe how I can tell you this story. Because life's instances are so complex and

VICTORY IN EUROPE

multifarious, it is impossible to capture the true essence of each moment in full detail. The best I can do is tell my tale as well as I can and hope I do so well enough for you to understand.

The human sacrifice cannot be fully described. It may never be completely understood, but the unforgettable memories, the fight for human life, the horrific suffering of this senseless and futile war should never again be repeated.

Every man, woman and child were affected in a multitude of ways by the havoc and misery the war brought and, when all the living memories fade and finally disappear, only cold, dispassionate historical records shall remain.

I feel this is one small and, possibly, my last chance to share with you my experience from a few days of May 1945. My story is one of courage and endurance in adversity, of compassion and, I reveal for the first time today, one of my love for Annie, my wartime pal and secret sweetheart.

VICTORY IN EUROPE

-o0o-

My friend, Annie, was walking towards me along the wall, placing one foot carefully in front of the other. When she reached me, she said, "Go on, Pat, your turn."

I walked to the far end, hoisted myself aloft, and carefully stood upright. The wall seemed far narrower than when simply sitting on it. I held my arms out until I steadied myself.

"Come on, Patricia. What are you waiting for?" Annie called out.

I walked forward, careful to step over the stumps of metal protruding through the coping stones at regular intervals.

Annie and I had, a few weeks ago, watched the men saw down the railings which sat atop this wall. The iron was needed to support the war effort. Not that we minded the men taking the railings as, once they were gone, we found a new game to play.

VICTORY IN EUROPE

A game of dare which went from simply walking along the top of the wall to skipping along it, then running, dancing and attempting amateur athletics like those shown in the newsreels at Saturday cinema. Not that Saturday cinema had been shown for a long time now.

When I reached Annie, we laughed and hugged. I settled on the wall next to her just as the Air Raid Warning sounded. Old Hitler was sending some more of his flying bombs over.

The first ones, Doodlebugs we called them, could be heard coming from a long way off. You were fairly safe all the time. You could hear their motors running, but once they stopped you had no idea where they would land. The waiting for the explosion was awfully frightening.

But these the rocket bombs, V2's, were almost silent. If you heard the 'whoomfph' of one landing, you knew you were okay. If you didn't hear it, you were either very far away or already dead.

VICTORY IN EUROPE

The wall was too far from the air raid shelter and much too far from home; where dear Daddy dug the garden and installed an Anderson Shelter with steps down and a canopy over. He made a sound wooden floor and a raised platform, where he placed a mattress to make sure it did not get damp.
We had a radio on the shelf. Electric light, camping stove, windproof matchsticks, kettle and tin mugs, along with all things for making tea and cocoa. It was very cosy. Even the cat would go down there.

I knew my mother would scurry to the shelter now, pulling my brother, Peter, along with her. She would worry about my whereabouts.
Most nights we slept in the shelter, although my diary records that on 6th November 1940 I slept in my bed. I still have no idea why.

I wonder about Daddy, and where he is now. It is six weeks since the last letters came. The Telegrams come. Each day, there is at least one delivered to the houses about our own. My cousin Norman was killed

VICTORY IN EUROPE

in France in a tank in 1944. My other cousin, his brother, is in the same regiment.

We ran to Aunt Mary's. She was not really an aunt to either Annie or me, but back then you addressed the people you knew, especially the ones who were friends of your parents, politely. Everyone I knew who was older than I was called Mr, Mrs, Uncle, or Aunt. It was the respectful thing to do, polite and proper.
I think Uncle Bill, Aunt Mary's husband, saw us running to the house. From an open front door, he called out, "Hurry girls," as he waved us forward.

The house was like many others along the street; all the windows were stuck with brown sticky tape in a cross pattern, in case the glass broke when the bombs fell.
Aunt Mary and Uncle Bill did not have a shelter in their garden, so we sat under the stairs. Annie and I snuggled close; our coats wrapped like cloaks about the both of us. We felt as long as we were together, we were safe.

VICTORY IN EUROPE

Aunt Mary has a small candle in a jar. The jar sits in a metal lid which is full of water. I think it strange but never mention it. On the back wall hangs a gas mask. It is black and has a green end. It smells. I think it feels like dead skin. I do never want to wear it.
After the All Clear, we walk home holding hands. I stand at the garden gate and wave to Annie as she carries on to Mrs Wilkinson's. She turns and waves back as she disappears around the unkempt privet hedge. Annie is an evacuee. This is her second time away from home. Because we live in the suburbs, her parents think she is safer here than in the city. I do not feel very safe, though.

"And where have you been?" Mother asked. She speaks quite sternly, but I can see the tension drain from her face and the dampness of relief in her eyes.
"We ran to Aunt Mary's and sat under the stairs," I told her, speaking as matter-of-factly as she.
"We?" she questioned.
"Annie and I," I said.

VICTORY IN EUROPE

"You can run an errand for me," she said, ignoring my answer. I took a pudding basin to the dripping shop. The queue stretched from the shop right to the end of the next road. I waited for ages until Mother came and said, "Don't wait any longer. There won't be any left by the time you get there."

It was dark along the Avenue as we walked home. The bushes looked ghostly. It was only the stars which peeped through the trees and there was very little light from them.

That night we, Mother, Peter and I, ate a special tea of jam sandwiches followed by tinned fruit. I would have liked some margarine on my bread, but as the rations were so small, it was always a choice of margarine or jam, never both.

We sprinkled a little dried milk powder over our tinned fruit. It makes the syrup taste creamy. One day, I have promised myself, I shall have some real cream. We had to go without many of life's basic essentials. Food rationing meant we only consumed what the

VICTORY IN EUROPE

weekly-allocated coupons permitted, so Mother created many weird and wondrous concoctions, some were nice, some passable and some horrid, but if you did not eat what was on your plate, you went without because there was nothing to replace it.

Luckily, Daddy planted rhubarb beside the Anderson shelter, gooseberries and currents along the garden wall. Mother tended the vegetable plot in his absence. This gave us fresh vegetables, some of which we swapped for other things, like eggs, which came from Mr Ridley's chickens at number 35.

Lying in bed that night, I could not help but notice how the lamppost outside my bedroom window was tall and dark, casting weird shadows across my windowpane and curtains. I wonder when the lamplighter will come back, and if the lamp will ever glow in the dark once again? I wish Annie was here to comfort me.

VICTORY IN EUROPE

My dream that night was of peeling and eating a banana. What a great joy that would be should it ever come true.

-o0o-

Mother promised we would visit Woolworths today. I was so excited because it is my favourite shop. When we arrived in the city centre, we saw Woolworths was bombed out.

There was glass and rubble everywhere and that strange smell of dust, concrete and something else, which I think came from the bombs. Someone said the city had taken a 'hell-of-a-pasting' over the last few days. It was very quiet for a place where children and grown-ups usually stand chatting and laughing.

There was little else we could do in town today, so, apart from Mother using a clothing coupon to buy some material from the haberdashers, we walked home. Mother preferred to spend her clothing coupons on material. She said you got more than if

VICTORY IN EUROPE

you bought ready-made clothing. Mother spent most evenings, once it was dark, sewing or knitting as she listened to the radio.

It was a quiet walk home. Neither of us spoke much at all.

I was so proud of Mother. She always tried to be cheerful. I remember her singing while she did the housework. She was a remarkable woman who possessed great fortitude, courage and determination. She was highly disciplined and, I often thought, harshly strict during my childhood but always very caring. She was a pillar of strength; without her, I know I would have felt much more fearful.

We arrived home around three o'clock that afternoon. Annie was waiting by the gate, hopping from one foot to the other. "Have you heard?" she called out excitedly, still waving at us, although we were only a few feet away.

"Heard what?" Mother asked.

VICTORY IN EUROPE

"They've surrendered. The wars over." Annie was shrugging, shaking her head and waving her arms about herself all at once. She made a strange sight.

We had hoped for an age the war would soon be over. In April, our Allied Forces met with the Russians who were fighting the Nazis on the Eastern front. Once Hitler realised the hopelessness of the situation, he killed himself.

"Are you certain, Annie?" Mother's head tilted to one side. It was something she did when trying to syphon the truth from gossip.

That evening, Monday the Seventh of May 1945, the BBC interrupted its scheduled programming with a news flash announcing Victory in Europe Day would be a national holiday.

That night, Mother and I made ginger biscuits for the street party. I shampooed my hair and went to bed at midnight. Tomorrow I was going to enjoy the celebrations with my dearest Annie.

-o0o-

VICTORY IN EUROPE

Tuesday, the Eighth of May 1945, was a warm and sunny day.
Annie and I boarded the train for London. We got off at Victoria and began, desperately, to make our way towards Buckingham Palace. We were astounded to see such a huge crowd. It was like a human wave staggering shoulder to shoulder along the mall. It was the most incredible sight. I doubt impassioned emotions will ever be as high again. London was aflame with exhilaration.

This was to be the end of suffering and hardship; peace finally descended upon us, and everybody was at one with each other regardless of race, creed, and status. Survival and freedom were all that mattered. We waited so very long for this and, in our wildest dreams, never envisaged a day like this.
After much effort, we finally reached Buckingham Palace. People were waving flags, drifting in from Piccadilly and Regent Street and thronging down the

mall. Most were singing their hearts out, particularly those favourites sung by Vera Lynn.

Bonfires were lit across the capital and fireworks streaked across the sky instead of searchlights and bombers. London became submerged in jubilation. People climbed on anything they could: statues, buildings, cars, every lamppost was scaled. Dustbin lids banged along with anything which would make a noise. Nothing mattered, only freedom, the hysterical crowds totally beyond any order.

The Royal family, along with Winston Churchill, came on to the balcony many times, joining the jubilation and joy. Each looked utterly exhilarated and thoroughly overwhelmed, as we all were in such an incredible atmosphere.

Wandering through the crowd, drinking beer and singing, Annie and I met two other girls. They said they were Lizbet and Maggie. We danced with them for a while and Lizbet threw her arms around me and kissed my cheek. Maggie took a swig from Annie's bottle of brown ale.

I mentioned how closely Lizbet looked like the princess Elizabeth. She said, "How very reassuring." After which, the jostling crowds parted us. It was only long after this day did the Palace reveal they allowed the princesses to secretly join in the celebrations. Now, no one believes I danced with (the then-future) Queen Elizabeth on VE day outside Buckingham Palace. They just think I am a stupid old woman with a silly made-up story, but it is the truth.

Of course, we lost all sense of time and when we got back to Victoria, the last trains had departed. We were not alone. There were many people on the platforms. We all laughed and talked and sang songs until we squeezed into the guard's van of the mail train. We all thought it a grand joke.

When the train stopped, we found the door on the side where we must alight was locked. Despite the guards searching, no key could be found to free us,

VICTORY IN EUROPE

so they lifted us, one by one, through the windows of the train. There were many shrieks of laughter and some lewd comments as our skirts caught and rode up above our knees. I know many men glanced at my stocking tops before I got to smooth my skirt down. It was all quite mad but the greatest fun. It seemed nothing mattered except that we had survived. After six long years of fear and sacrifice, we were at last totally free. We had lived through it all. No words I say can really describe the intense feelings of relief on that night of celebration and jubilation. Strangers kissed strangers and everyone hugged everyone. The experience will be with me forever.

It was a strange sight walking home from the station, to witness the streets ablaze with light for the first time since 1939. Lampposts were lit, shop windows glowed, and lights shone through the windows of every home. It was like walking into a dream world. The town band and the Salvation Army band were playing up and down the streets and endless lines of those doing the 'Conga' danced in and out of every house. Mr Brown set up his barrel organ and continued playing all our favourite great war songs. No one wanted the night to end and, if Annie and I had our way, it never would have.

Annie left a few days after VE-day. I stood alone on the station platform with tears streaming down my face, waving goodbye as the train moved off through billowing smoke and steam.
I never saw my sweet Annie again, although the visions of her come uncontrollably flooding back each time I hear the song 'You'll Never Know.'

-o0o-

Epilogue

Daddy came home a few weeks later; he was invalided out of the army. He was thin, ill, and very grumpy. Luckily for Mother, she did not have to nurse him all herself. We had two nurses who came to billet with us. They worked at the city hospital. There were

VICTORY IN EUROPE

so many nurses and too few living quarters we got to share our home with Edna, a rather large round-faced girl, and Jean, a petite girl from Yorkshire. They both helped Mother with Daddy, although they did not need to.

A short time later, the girls moved into the hospital's nurses' quarters. Daddy was slowly getting better and was now on 'light-duties', attending the vegetable garden and undertaking some small household repairs. Jean still came to see us frequently, inquiring about Daddy's recovery. As Daddy got better, Jean's visits continued. It soon became clear she was visiting me.

Jean and I remained friends and shared a home from 1952. Locally, we were known as the 'spinster sisters', which suited us fine as our liaison was not one which was as publicly acceptable as such relationships are nowadays.

I saw much suffering during the war. Many times we reached the zenith of fear, times when there was hardly a glimmer of light pervading our darkness. The experience made me compassionate to others who are less fortunate. I learnt to be appreciative, to be philosophical, and to have courage and endurance in the face of adversity. As children, even in peacetime, we were taught always to be grateful for what we had. The war certainly highlighted this.

These are a few of my memories. I pray you never experience anything so devastating.
Jean died twenty years ago, leaving me alone in a world I no longer recognise, or can call my own. I often wonder what it was all for.

VICTORY IN EUROPE

I dedicate this story to the White Butterflies.

"Most remarkable of all was the appearance of many thousands of white butterflies which fluttered around. It was as if the souls of the dead soldiers had come to haunt the spot where so many fell. It was eerie to see them, and the silence. It was so still I could almost hear the beat of the butterflies' wings."

VICTORY IN EUROPE

VICTORY IN EUROPE

BUTTERFLIES OF DUNKIRK

BY CLAIRE PLAISTED

All shapes and sizes of vessels left the English ports. Any seaworthy boat went to rescue those from the French shores and the horror of the massacre on Dunkirk. The boats approached the French shoreline, fear on the faces of the captains and sailors, as they watched the slaughter continue. The boats powered ahead to rescue as many men as they could, praying for the souls of those they couldn't.

Close enough now, men were running towards them, guns firing, some toppled dead in the water having been shot before they could get to the boats.
Big black bursts of smoke appeared overhead, where Spitfires and Messerschmitt fought aggressively in a massive dogfight. The Spitfires were in protection

mode; the Messerschmitts doing what damage they could.

British, American, and Canadian men fell in their thousands. The captains hauled those they could into boats of all shapes and sizes.
With their vessels full, they pulled away as other boats took their places. It was a constant movement on the ocean waves.
Some of the men looked back, watching the massacre, many knowing they'd never see some of their comrades again. They saluted the fallen men.
Just as they ended, thousands of different coloured butterflies rose into the sky, disappearing into the horizon.
The souls of men.

Dedicated to Greg Sadler with love.

ROSEMARY FOR REMEMBRANCE

BY JULIA BLAKE

All day long, the sounds of revelry in the streets had increased until by going home time it sounded as if every citizen of London was out there celebrating. As the noise level rose, so had Veronica's excitement, and Rosemary could see her friend twitching in her seat, her fingers tapping with barely contained anticipation on the keys.

Finally, it was 5pm and Mr Finnegan glanced up at them as they rose and put the covers over their typewriters.

"Go straight home now, girls," he ordered. "Things are going to get a little wild out there tonight, so best you get home as quickly as you can."

"Yes, Mr Finnegan," they chorused, leaving the office and sedately closing the door behind them.

Veronica turned to Rosemary, her eyes shining with excitement.

"Ladies, now" she muttered and clutched Rosemary's hand, her palm clammy with excitement as she dragged her half reluctant friend towards the lavatories at the end of the corridor.

The plan had been explained to Rosemary during their dinner break. No way were they going straight home, Veronica had declared, her eyes bright with anticipation. No way. History was being made out there tonight, and they needed to be a part of it.

Rosemary had agreed, well, she always agreed with Veronica. Slightly in awe of her older, more worldly friend, Rosemary was the quiet one who tagged along with whatever madcap scheme Veronica had cooked

VICTORY IN EUROPE

up, happy that such an exciting and glamorous person was her friend. And Veronica was glamorous. Everyone thought so.

With her Veronica Lake curls and pouting red lips, she was the personification of Hollywood glamour, although Rosemary's mother had sniffed and wondered aloud precisely how she managed to get an endless supply of stockings, lipstick, and chocolate. Her tone suggested she had a strong suspicion of exactly how.

Rosemary knew where V got these highly desirable items. She knew because Veronica had confided in her that she saved her favours for one young American airman in particular, fully confident of a proposal and a one-way ticket to the States when the war was over.
Well, now it was over, the war in Europe anyway. The guns had fallen silent, and their soldiers would come home, including…

VICTORY IN EUROPE

"Have you heard from George lately?" Veronica broke into her train of thought, her eyes almost crossing as she applied a thick layer of Vaseline to her eyelashes and gently elongated them with her fingertips.

"George? No, not since that last letter two months ago."

"He'll be home soon, I expect," Veronica eyed her beadily as she held her lips apart and applied a thick layer of red lipstick. "And then you'll have to give him an answer. You told him you couldn't even think about it until the war was over, and I get that, but the war is now over, and all our boys will come home. So, what are you going to tell him?"

"I don't know," Rosemary stared at her reflection in the mirror and listlessly pulled a comb through her own lacklustre hair, wishing it looked like V's, wishing she was more like Veronica.

"Do you love him?"

"I like George a lot."

"That's not what I asked," Veronica snapped the lid back on the lipstick and dropped it into her bag, patting her own curls with a smug air of satisfaction that had Rosemary eyeing her mousy locks in the mirror again, and sighing.

"Well?" Veronica asked again.
"I don't know," Rosemary admitted.
"Then you don't," Veronica declared knowledgeably.
"When you're in love, you know you're in love."
"Like you and Andrew?" Rosemary asked shyly.

She'd met Andrew once or twice, and had been overwhelmed by his brash American manners, his confidence, and devil-may-care attitude to the war and the fact he could die any day.
"Yes," Veronica paused in her titivations and stared levelly at Rosemary in the mirror. "When I met him, I just knew that he was the one."
"Is that why you… you know…?"
"Had sex with him?" Veronica smirked at Rosemary's flushed face. "It was that, and the fact that life is so uncertain right now. We knew every night we had together could be our last, so we were determined to

make it count for something. And that's why I'm saying if you were truly in love with George, you wouldn't have made him wait.

Now come on, let's get out there before old Fussy Finnegan orders us straight home again."

Veronica had arranged for them to meet Andrew and his friends, and as they emerged onto the street, blinking in the warm rays of the May early evening sunshine, Rosemary felt a sudden surge of apprehension.
"Maybe I should go home," she began, but Veronica just laughed and took her by the hand.
"No getting cold feet now," she ordered. "We're going to have some fun at last!"

And it was fun. To begin with. The streets were heaving with people, so many people, all determined to celebrate this most wonderful occasion. The war was over. All those long, bitter years they'd suffered through had finally ended. Barely twelve years old

VICTORY IN EUROPE

when it all began, Rosemary could hardly remember what it had been like before.

When her parents reminisced about having plenty of food and being able to walk the streets at night with no fear of bombs dropping, she'd felt it was another world they were describing. A magical land of safety and plenty.

Andrew and his friends had acquired beer from somewhere and were openly swigging it on the streets, and nobody cared. Looking around, Rosemary saw food and drink being shared amongst friends and strangers alike. One young airman offered her a swig of his beer and she took it, not liking the sour gassy taste, but desperately wanting to be part of it all. It settled in her empty stomach, spreading a warm glow throughout her body, and she laughed with the others.

They allowed themselves to be swept along with the crowds, surging inwards to the heart of the city, until suddenly the familiar shape of Nelson's Column towered above them, and Rosemary realised they'd reached Trafalgar Square.

People were in the fountains, and Rosemary saw Veronica's mouth open in a shriek as Andrew swept her off her feet and stood her on the stone surround, threatening to push her in.
"Wait, wait," she laughed, and quickly bent to pull off her shoes. Rosemary knew they were her best ones – she wouldn't want them to get ruined. Then she was in the water, her skirts clutched to her thighs, revealing long shapely legs and a hint of stocking tops and garters. The watching men cheered. Andrew grinned with pride, and Veronica dimpled her pleasure at their admiration.

"Come on in, Rosemary," she ordered, but Rosemary shook her head. Too shy to reveal her bare legs to all these men, not having V's endless supply of stockings or her endless legs, she merely watched and smiled as Veronica clung to Andrew's arm and posed for a

VICTORY IN EUROPE

man with a camera who was taking pictures of the crowd.

They moved on, Veronica laughingly complaining about her wet feet, but not really caring. It wasn't a night for caring about anything.
The crowds grew as more people got off work and joined the thronging masses. Voices rose as one and Rosemary felt tears start to her eyes at a rousing rendition of her favourite song, "We'll Meet Again", that was being belted out through an open pub door.

Trailing along behind the group, content to linger on the outskirts, she was to tongue-tied to respond to the attempts of Andrew's friends to bring her into their celebration. Eventually, they gave up trying, merely handing her beer to drink and smiling at her.

She stumbled over her own feet. Looking down, she saw the laces on her sensible shoes, which had been repaired so many times there was practically no original leather left on them, had come undone.

VICTORY IN EUROPE

Swiftly, she dropped to her knee to tie it, the crowd parting around her like a rock mid-current in a stream. When she arose, she looked for her group. They were gone. Trying to calm her pounding heart, she was swept along by the tide of bodies, her eyes looking for Veronica's shining curls, or Andrew's height, for anyone that looked familiar.

There was no sign of them. She was alone.
It doesn't matter, she told herself fiercely. Go home, you've had your fun. You've experienced that moment in history Veronica had been talking about, and you've got something to tell your grandchildren.

Turning, she tried to push back through the crowds to find her way to an underground station and make her long way home. The crowd pushed back. Too large a mass for one slight woman to make an impression on, she was buffeted and shoved, her feeble pleas to be allowed through unheard and ignored.

VICTORY IN EUROPE

Panic began to rise. It was all too much. This mass of people had taken on a sinister life of its own. Intent on merrymaking, its needs brutally crushed her own desperate desire to be free of it.

"Please," she cried. "Please, let me through." Somewhere far up ahead, music blared, and the crowd surged forward in eager anticipation. Crying out in panic, Rosemary's ankle twisted beneath her, and with a shocked yelp she fell to the road, her knee impacting on the hard surface and her wrist bending back painfully as she attempted to stop her fall.

Someone trod on her hand, a leg knocked violently into the side of her head, and her bag was wrenched from her grasp. Scrabbling furiously on the ground, Rosemary clutched desperately at its strap and yanked it back into her body, horribly afraid of losing it in the stampeding crush.

"Hey, you okay?"

VICTORY IN EUROPE

Next moment, strong arms were lifting her up and a male body was sheltering her. Her heart pounding with fear, Rosemary looked up into the laughing blue eyes of her rescuer. They twinkled back. A grin creased a cheery, boyishly handsome face as he continued to steady her with one hand at her elbow, the other on the small of her back.

"Ma'am, are you okay?" he asked again, and Rosemary looked down at herself. Her knee was bleeding, as was the heel of her hand, and she held it up in mute reply. His grin dropped, and he looked around at the uncaring masses.

"Over here," he said, and somehow managed to push his way through the crowds, dragging her along with him. Dumbly, she clung to his side allowing him to lead the way, the crowds miraculously parting in the face of his determined but polite passage.
"Excuse me, coming through, injured lady here, please let us through."

VICTORY IN EUROPE

Eventually, they reached the pavement, and he steered her into a pub. Already packed with revellers, he nevertheless manged to find them a tiny table tucked in the corner and deposited her gently on a chair.

"Stay here," he ordered, then was swallowed up in the crowd around the bar, which was waiting to be served.

He was gone for ages - long enough for her knee and hand to start throbbing and for her to begin thinking about simply going and trying to find her way home by herself. But the noise and crush outside the door was enough to make her shudder and sink back into the relative security of her seat.

"Here you go."

He was back, bearing a tray full of things - a bowl of water, a clean cloth, a tube of antiseptic salve, and two glasses of something.

"Thank you."

She finally spoke to him, her shock having abated enough for her to notice his American accent and the

VICTORY IN EUROPE

dark brown of his uniform jacket. She knew that
meant he was Air Force, like Andrew and his friends,
and wondered why he was out alone.
"It's very kind of you to help me."
"Couldn't ignore a damsel in distress," he replied and
twinkled that smile at her again. "Why are you out
alone, though? It's rough out there tonight."

"I was with friends," she began. "We got separated,
and I was trying to go home but I was knocked over."
"You're lucky they didn't trample right over you. I don't
think anyone is thinking very clearly tonight."
"No," she agreed, wincing as she washed the gravel
from her knee and hand, tenderly dabbed them dry,
then smeared antiseptic cream on them.

"You should be fine," he reassured her. "It's just a bit
of gravel rash. It'll be okay by the morning."
"Thank you, again," she smiled at him. "It's very kind
of you to help me this way."
He shrugged, then handed her one of the glasses.
"Brandy," he told her.

VICTORY IN EUROPE

"Oh, but I don't like…"

"It's medicinal," he stated firmly. "So, get it down you."

Obediently, she sipped at the syrupy liquid. Just like the beer earlier, its warmth hit her stomach, then immediately spread throughout her body.

"I'm Charles," he said and held out a hand over the table. "But all my friends call me Charlie."

"Rosemary," she replied and took his hand, his palm warm against hers.

"Do your friends call you anything else?"

"No, just Rosemary," she said, reluctant to confess that apart from Veronica she had no other friends.

With a clutch of realisation, Rosemary wondered how much V had worried when she realised Rosemary was no longer with them. Probably not much, she thought sadly.

"Well, I shall call you Rosie," Charlie declared.

Rosemary's cheeks bloomed with sudden heat. It was the brandy, she told herself fiercely. It couldn't possibly be from anything else.

"It means remembrance," she informed him.

"What does?"

"My name, Rosemary. It's Rosemary for remembrance."

"I don't think I'll need any help remembering you,"

Charlie stated with a cocky grin over the rim of his glass. "And you're too little for such a big name. I like Rosie better."

She smiled shyly and buried her face in her glass. On renewed acquaintance, the brandy didn't taste so bad and slipped down easier than the first sip.

"Why are you here alone, then?" she asked.

"Oh, I was with a group of guys but all they wanted to do was drink and I wanted to look around and simply be part of it all. You know, this is really important. It's like it's…"

VICTORY IN EUROPE

"A moment in history?" she finished his sentence and was gratified when he slowly nodded.

"That's right," he agreed, then threw down the last of his drink and set the glass down with a decisive thud. "So, shall we?"

"Shall we what?" she asked in confusion.

"Go and experience this moment in history?"

"What, together you mean?"

"Sure, why not? I mean, you've temporarily misplaced your friends and I've dumped mine for the night. So why don't we go and look for your friends, and along the way we'll have some fun."

Rosemary stared at him, her heart beating so loudly she was sure everyone could hear it over the din of the crowded pub. Charlie grinned again, that wide-mouthed, disarming smile of his that was already so achingly familiar.

"Okay," she agreed slowly, the slang word sharp on her tongue. "If you wouldn't mind helping me look for my friends, that would be wonderful, thank you." But a small part of her hoped they'd never find Veronica, or at least that it would take a very long time.

They went back to Trafalgar Square, Charlie insisting the best way to start the search for Veronica and her group was to go back to the last place she'd seen them. A band of sorts was now playing, and people were dancing in the historic space. With a whoop of joyful laughter, Charlie pulled her by the hand, and they were in the thick of the dancers.

Veronica had tried unsuccessfully to teach Rosemary how to dance, laughing rather unkindly at her friend's two left feet. But now, with Charlie's warm hands holding and guiding her, his grin flashing encouragement, Rosemary found her feet moving by themselves as she jitterbugged and grooved with the best of them.

Throwing her head back in utter abandonment, Rosemary was lost in the sensations of the moment, caught up in a collective euphoria that swept through

VICTORY IN EUROPE

the crowd and united them in shared emotions of relief and happiness.

They left the square, searching for other amusements. An enterprising fish & chip shop had quickly fired up the fryers and was selling portions of chips in twists of newspaper. Charlie bought them one to share, and Rosemary laughed in disbelief at the amount of vinegar he drenched the chips with.

"What?" he exclaimed as she shook vinegar from her fingers. "I've got a taste for it now. We don't have this back home."

"Where is home?" she asked.

"Memphis, Tennessee," he replied, but the names meant nothing to her, and she only shook her head and laughed in return.

Then they were running with the crowd again; more music, more dancing, and every time she looked at Charlie, she wanted to explode with happiness. A tiny, sensible voice in her brain was insisting she take

care, that this was only temporary. It couldn't,
wouldn't, last the night. When dawn came and chased
away the night, so too would it chase him away.
But for once Rosemary didn't want to be sensible.
Drunk on adrenalin, she clung to his hand and
followed where he led, and still the night went on.

Darkness fell and for the first time in five years, light
blazed on the streets. The crowd cheered and
Rosemary realised how much she'd hated the
blackout; the fear of being outside after dusk had
fallen; the menace she'd always suspected lurked in
the gloom of London's dim streets.

They'd given up any pretence of looking for Veronica,
and Charlie was showing no signs of wanting the
evening to end. Like her, he seemed intent on merely
existing in the moment. The smell of hot chips with
too much vinegar. The tang of the cheap wine from
the bottle that someone shared with them. The blare
of music as people gathered with instruments
wherever there was a space and began to play. The

dancing that was without structure or form but instead flowed from squares and parks and out into the avenues and streets.

They tasted it all. Every sensation there was on offer that evening, they tried. Some of the fancy hotels on the posher side of the city had thrown open their doors for the night. The crowd mingled, the common rubbing shoulders with the elite, and nobody caring, all barricades and distinction suspended for one glorious night.

They drank cocktails in a hotel bar that had a giant mirror behind it and Rosemary caught a glimpse of herself, shocked by the beautiful woman who laughed and sparkled Charlie's arm around her waist as they clinked glasses.

She couldn't stop touching him. They couldn't stop touching each other. Laughing into each other's eyes, his hand would brush her cheek and stroke her hair.

His mouth close to her face as he said something in her ear.

They finished their drinks and left their glasses on the bar. Taking her by the hand, Charlie pulled her backwards into the crowd and eased her into the safe harbour of his arms. He was warm and smelt of the gin he'd just drunk, and vinegar from the chips. But underneath that she could smell him, a fresh male citrus scent that filled up her senses with a giddy intoxication.

Unable to hear what music was coming from the direction of the hotel's ballroom, they swayed on the spot to their own rhythm. One of his hands held hers, the other was firm on the small of her back, and Rosemary had never felt so protected and cherished in all her life.
His breath tickled on her cheek and then he was humming something in her ear. It was, "We'll Meet Again".

VICTORY IN EUROPE

"That's my favourite song," she exclaimed, and he smiled at her with his eyes.

"And mine," he said.

They stopped and stared at one another, the thrill of connection throbbing through their young bodies that were already drunk on the heightened emotions charging through the crowd like electricity.

Tenderly, he cupped her face in his hand. The look in his eyes was enough to make her cry, and she tried to swallow past the heart-shaped lump in her throat. Looking back, Rosemary supposed under the circumstances it was inevitable what happened next.

Caught up in the wild maelstrom of emotions, all bets were off, all inhibitions quashed, and when he kissed her, as she'd hoped - oh so desperately hoped he would – she'd not only let him, she'd kissed him back and she'd known. Just as Veronica had said she would, she'd known.

VICTORY IN EUROPE

Wolf whistles and catcalls erupted around them as the mob good-humouredly applauded their embrace.

"Tell her you love her, mate," one inebriated young soldier yelled to Charlie, slapping him amiably on the back.
Charlie drew away from the kiss and stared into her face. His grin had dropped, and her heart hurt at the look in his eyes. Suddenly serious, he pulled her out into the foyer of the hotel.

"Rosie," he began helplessly, and she shook his arm. "It's alright," she said and laughed nervously. "He was only joking. It doesn't matter."
"No, it does matter," he insisted. "And I know it's crazy, but I think I do. I do love you, Rosie. But how can that be so quickly? I mean, it's crazy, right?"
"Yes," she agreed. "It is crazy, but I don't care, because I love you, too."
"We're shipping back to the States tomorrow," he said. "But if I send for you, will you come?"

VICTORY IN EUROPE

"Yes," she said immediately, all thoughts of her family, her job, George, flying from her mind.

There was only Charlie and the way he was looking at her and the way her heart ached at the thought of saying goodbye to him.

She remembered what Veronica had said - if you know it could be your last night, you make it count - and her eyes fell on the racks of room keys behind the desk. Quickly, not giving herself time to think, she slipped around the desk and grabbed the first key she saw. Charlie's eyes widened as she hurried back to his side and showed him the key.

"Rosie," he began, "are you certain?"
"Yes," she said and kissed him again. "I've never been more certain of anything in my life."
It was a nice room, but it really wouldn't have mattered what kind of room it was because there was only him, and only her, and the rest of the world had gone away. It was his first time too, he told her, and

she believed him, and if their first time together was fine, the second time was even better.

They lay together as dawn crept through the undrawn curtains and made plans. He had to go back to the States, that was inevitable, but they would write, and as soon as possible he would send for her and they would get married at his family's home.

Would that be alright?
Yes. She agreed to everything, to all of it, needing to hear him say the words, desperately wanting reassurances that this was a dream that must come true.

They were engaged; he promised her and took a gold crucifix off from around his neck and placed it around hers. He didn't have a ring and there was no time to get one, but this was a family heirloom, something he'd never give away lightly. This showed how serious he was.

VICTORY IN EUROPE

She held it in her hand, its edges sharp in her palm, and she believed him. Holding him as closely as she could, her fingers played on his neck now bare of the chain, and for the first time she saw the heart shaped pink birthmark at the top of his spine.

"Oh, that's kind of a family heirloom as well," he admitted. "A lot of us in my family have it, so I guess at least one of our children will have it, and even our grandchildren."

Children, grandchildren… she clutched at his words the way a drowning man grabs for a rope, and she believed him.

Then it was the next day, and it had to be faced. Sneaking out of the hotel down the backstairs, they emerged into a city hungover from the night before.

People slept where they had fallen, slumped in doorways singly and together, and a few hardy souls still partied on. Holding tightly to Charlie's hand, Rosemary suddenly wondered about her parents, about how they must have worried when she didn't come home last night.

"Shall we see if we can find some breakfast?" he asked. "There's a café near here that me and the boys sometimes go to."
She nodded, wanting to stretch the time she had with him to as many hours, minutes, and seconds as she could.
"We'll get pen and paper in the café," he continued, "and you can give me your address and I'll give you mine."
They turned onto the main street in front of the hotel as a large crowd of determined revellers suddenly swept down upon them with the force of a riptide. Rosemary stumbled and her hand was violently torn from his.

"Charlie!" she screamed, trying to stand still and scan the crowd around her. "Charlie! No, please, stop, let me go back." But it was no use. The sheer force of the crowd carried her the entire length of the road until she managed to shove her way to the edge and emerged, breathless and shaking, onto the pavement.

She stood still, waiting for him to find her, expecting at any moment he'd erupt from the crowd, his blue eyes looking for her. She imagined the relief on his face when he saw her, the way he'd rush to her and catch her up in his arms. Then he'd take her to the café, and they'd swap addresses and she'd be safe.

"Charlie," she whispered. "Please."
She waited. It felt like hours. Eventually, when the crowd had abated enough for her to risk it, she plunged back in and fought her way to the hotel and tried to get back in. But the doors were shut and locked and no one answered her frantic hammering, and anyway, what would she tell them? What could she say? That he had been hers for a night and now he was gone?

Her face burned with shame as she imagined what they would think, what they would imply. Silly little tart, to be fooled so easily by a Yank when everyone knew what they were like, only after one thing. Well, she'd given it to him and now he was gone, and she had no idea where to look for him.

Not knowing what else to do, she sat on the hotel steps for over an hour before finally, reluctantly, she went home.

-o0o-

Although she was the oldest resident of the Cedar Pines Care Home, she never seemed to lack for visitors and today was no exception. As her eldest great-grandson and his young wife carefully carried their four-week-old baby daughter up to her sunny room, staff and other residents alike smiled and cooed at the tiny pink bundle that stared out at the world through unfocused blue eyes.

"Hello, Nana Rose."

He gently tapped at the half-opened door, his face peering enquiringly through the gap. Eagerly, the elderly lady in the bed put down the book she'd been reading and held out her arms in anticipation.

"Anthony," she exclaimed happily. "Darling Liv. And this must be the newest member of the family."

"It is," he said, taking the small pink bundle from his wife and sitting gently on the edge of his great-grandmother's bed. "Nana Rose, I'd like you to meet Charlotte Rosemary, your new great-great-granddaughter."

Softly, he lay his tiny daughter into her wrinkled arms and she held the bundle close, peering down into the scrunched-up little face, the lines on her cheeks relaxing into a smile of love and joy. She glanced up at her great-grandson and his wife.

"She has your nose Anthony, but your smile Liv, and that means she's absolutely perfect." Gently, her fingers parted the shawl and stroked down the child's neck, her fingers pausing at the base. "Oh, does she have…?"

"The family birthmark?" continued Anthony and grinned. "She does, Nana Rose. A perfect little pink heart. So funny how it skips the generations. I mean, Dad didn't have it, but Grandpa Gordon did. Did great-grandpa George have it?"

"No," his great-grandmother's eyes clouded slightly. "He didn't have it." She looked down at the baby again. "Charlie," she whispered.

"Charlotte," Liv corrected her. "Although, I like Charlie and I guess it's inevitable her name will get shortened to that."

"So, what do you think Nana Rose?" Anthony stooped and took the baby back, holding her upright so she could study her great-great-grandmother. "Does she have the family look?"

"Oh yes," came the soft reply. "She looks just like your great-great-grandfather."

"I wish I'd known great-grandpa George," Anthony continued. "What was he like?"

"George?" she paused to consider the question.

VICTORY IN EUROPE

"My husband, George was without a doubt the most forgiving and kind-hearted man that ever lived." She stopped, her mind going back to that dreadful day, so long, long ago now, when she'd stood in front of a young man who loved her and told him why she couldn't marry him.

Drowning in tears, she'd admitted everything that had happened and the consequences that were now hers, and hers alone, to bear. Shocked and hurt beyond belief, he'd left, slamming the door so hard her parents had hurried in from the kitchen to see what was up, their dismay and anger growing when she'd cried hysterically and told them of the shame their beloved daughter was about to bring down on their family.

But George had come back. Walking the streets of London for many lonely hours, he'd considered everything and realised that he still loved her. Loved her enough to marry her and take on another man's child and to never, not once, reproach her for it or hold it against her.

And as the years passed and Gordon remained their only child, she had seen how much he had come to love the boy, as if he was his own flesh and blood, and they'd never told anyone any differently.

They'd been happy together, and she had genuinely grieved when he'd died the year before their great-grandson Anthony had been born.

"Yes," she nodded her head. "My husband, George was a wonderful man," she paused and looked at Anthony, "but your great-grandfather was the love of my life."

A flicker of confusion passed over Anthony's face, then he smiled at her and handed the baby back to his wife.

"We'll let you get some rest, Nana Rose, but we'll be back to see you soon, and of course there'll be the christening to arrange."

VICTORY IN EUROPE

As he bent to press a kiss on her soft scented cheeks, she clung to him, her frail hands clutching at his arms with a strength that belied her apparent fragility.

"I love you," she murmured. "I just wanted you to know that."

"Love you too, Nana Rose," he reassured her.

When they'd gone, the old lady in the bed fumbled in the drawer of her bedside cabinet and withdrew a small velvet pouch. Her twisted fingers struggling with a knot that hadn't been undone in decades, she persevered and finally tipped the contents into her lap.

"Charlie," she murmured, and held the gold crucifix up to catch the bright, mid-morning sun that was streaming through her window. "Charlie, my love, so many years, oh so many years."

"I looked for you, Rosie."

Startled, she wiped at his eyes, dimmed with tears and peered at the barely-there shape in the corner of the room.

"Charlie?"

"When I lost you in the crowd, I searched everywhere for you. I went back to the hotel and waited there for ages, but you never came.

Then I looked all along the street, but you were gone, and I didn't know how to find you. I didn't even know your name and didn't have the first clue how to start looking for you. Then I had to go back to America, but I came back to Britain the first chance I had, and I looked for you. For four years, every summer, I came back to London and looked for you. But I never found you, and in the end my family convinced me that it was hopeless."

"I know," she nodded in agreement, the tears streaming down her parchment cheeks. "I know, my love. Perhaps we never had a chance, not really, to be together."
"I tried to make the best of my life, Rosie, but I never forgot you."
"I never forgot you either, Charlie."
"And I never stopped loving you, Rosie."

VICTORY IN EUROPE

"Oh Charlie, my Charlie. Have you come to get me?"
"Yes, it's time now, my love, time for us to finally be together."

He held out his hand and suddenly she was his Rosie again, young and smooth skinned, with feet that could dance all night and still have the energy for more. Eagerly, she reached for him and their fingers touched, and their hands grasped and there was only him and there was only her, and the rest of the world had gone away.

The crucifix slipped from her fingers to land on the floor where it would later be found by a member of staff, and that, together with the beautiful smile on her face, comforted her family a little. Saddened by their loss, they reassured themselves that although Nana Rose had died alone, at the end she'd been smiling. And after all, that was the way she would have wished to be remembered.

VICTORY IN EUROPE

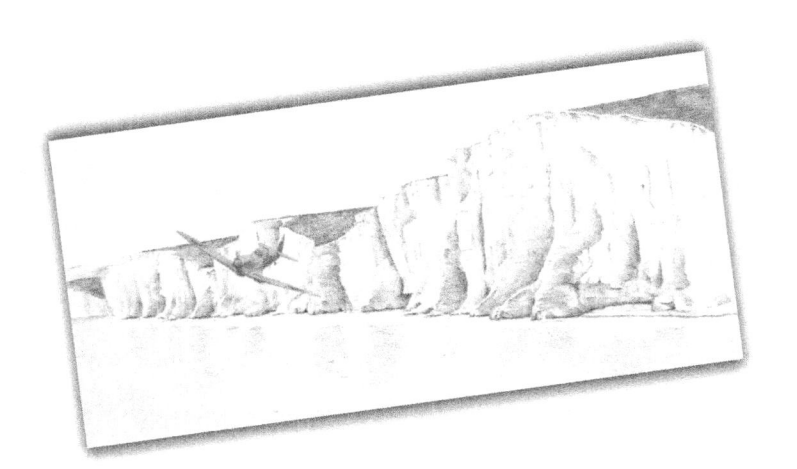

VICTORY IN EUROPE

WE'LL MEET AGAIN

BY JANE RISDON

What a day! Mavis kicked off her shoes, undid her suspenders, carefully rolling her stockings down her tired legs and over her aching feet. She sighed loudly as she placed her feet in the tin bath filled with hot water from the large copper kettle permanently simmering on the blackened kitchen range.

The street party trestles had been cleared away along with the bunting and leftovers from the VE Day celebrations. The men had wandered off to the pub to continue their drinking whilst mothers had taken their over-tired off-spring home to bed. All was quiet for a change. Her ears ached with the silence, but she closed her eyes and enjoyed the warmth of the water as the Epsom Salts soothed her pain away.

It's over, she mused, wiggling her toes and laying back against the sagging sofa. Six long years of war over, just like that. A group of old men decided, and it ended just like that!

Mavis thought of all her friends and locals whose brothers, sons, and husbands had died or were still missing, like her Bert. A telegram arrived a few months ago telling of 'their' regret in informing her that her husband was 'missing in action,' believed dead.

Dead? The word rattled around her brain for days before she allowed herself to speak the words out loud: Bert. Dead. Missing. What did 'missing in action' really mean? What action? Who said so? But she didn't believe it, she wouldn't. Her Bert, gone, never to be seen again. Never? She'd know – surely - if he'd ceased to be.

VICTORY IN EUROPE

The warmth of the water relaxed her. Soon her eyes began to droop, and Mavis began to drift off to sleep. Bert wandered into her mind and she recalled their first meeting at the Agincourt Dance Hall one Sunday afternoon when the WI hosted tea dances for the locals and the various troops stationed at Black Down camp. It was exciting meeting so many young men at one go. Usually, the only men she and her friends encountered were the local lads they'd grown up with. There were only about a hundred families in the village and living on the nearby farms, so inevitably - having such a limited selection of future mates - relationships were formed between those who had grown up together.

But Mavis did not want inevitable, she wanted excitement, a change. A new life. She wanted to see the world, to travel and to live life to the full. When her pals married their second or third cousins or old school friends, she was happy for them. Of course she was, but she felt sad for them and their limited horizons and ambitions. Mavis was determined to make something of herself, to get away from the village and to see the world.

The Agincourt was her portal to another world, and she went every Sunday with a sense of excitement and anticipation. Her escape route had to be waiting for her there and she was determined not to miss the opportunity when it came knocking, as she was sure it would.

-o0o-

Stanley Potter's Band played Vera Lynn's, 'We'll Meet Again,' as Mavis and her best friend Agnes sipped their tea from canteen style white China cups, their eyes watching the latest arrivals from the camp. Both girls were wearing their Sunday best and wore their hair in the latest style, which they'd created for each other on Friday night whilst they listened to the BBC Forces programme.

'Mavis, did you see the tall bloke who looks like Michael Rennie, the one near the exit?' Agnes nudged Mavis in the ribs and nodded towards the double exit doors.

'What? Oh yes, he does look like him. Uncanny,' her friend replied, but it soon became apparent that Mavis was staring at another bloke who'd just come in on his own.

The soldier was tall, dressed as the others were, in uniform, but for some reason he carried himself differently and stood out from the others. Agnes was impressed but she wasn't attracted to him like she was the Rennie look alike. Mavis noticed he didn't appear to be with anyone else, male or female, which pleased her for some reason.

'Yours is a bit of all right, Mavis, but mine's a cracker. See you later.' And Agnes walked over to the man of her dreams and brazenly asked him for a dance. Mavis realised her friend had gone just as the soldier she was staring at caught her eye and winked. She

VICTORY IN EUROPE

blushed and looked at her shoes; good grief, he'd seen her staring. She wanted the floor to open and swallow her. Too late. He was on his way over to her. 'Hello.' He stood in front of her, his eyes dancing with mischief and obvious enjoyment at her discomfort.

'Hello,' she replied, and blushed an even deeper shade of red. Get a grip, Mavis, she thought, as her eyes met his. They were a deep topaz blue, she noticed.

'Do you come here often?' He said, and then burst out laughing at the look of horror on her face. 'Sorry, I didn't mean it to come out like that,' he chuckled, and Mavis couldn't help herself. She giggled too.

He hoped she'd not seen him when he'd been in before. That would've been most unfortunate. The soldier grinned sheepishly at her, working his magic. 'Hardly original, but yes, I do. I come with my friend Agnes. She's the girl in the grey dress dancing with Michael Rennie.' She pointed to her friend, who winked at her when she passed by in the arms of her movie star look-alike.

VICTORY IN EUROPE

'Want to dance?' He grabbed her arm before she could answer and dragged her on to the floor, wrapping his arms around her and moving in time with the music.

The afternoon passed quickly as Mavis and the soldier danced every dance together. They chatted comfortably, and he told her his name was Bert, and he was expecting to be deployed any time soon. He was an orphan having grown up in the care of an aunt until she died, and then he was sent to The Duke of York's Royal Military School for the children of military personnel in Kent, because his father had been in the military when he died.

Mavis told him she lived in the village of Sandhurst, not far from the Agincourt. Bert knew all about the Royal Military College, Sandhurst (RMC, Sandhurst), the grounds of which came up to the edge of the road opposite the Agincourt. It was where Officer Cadets received their training. It was out of his league. He'd never aspired to be an officer, he told her. Too much responsibility, besides you had to be posh with bucket loads of money to go to Sandhurst.

'Dad worked at the Staff College until he died two years ago. He got gassed in the Big War and was always ill after; his lungs, you know. Mum died not long after him.' Mavis blinked away the tears which always came when she spoke of her parents. 'I've got Mum's uncle, but otherwise I'm on my tod too.'
'Here, wipe your eyes.' Bert handed her his handkerchief, which she took. 'I didn't mean to upset you,' he added, concern etched on his handsome face, filing away all she said in his memory. You never knew.
'Not your fault. I'm daft getting myself all upset, sorry. You must think I'm soft.'
'Not at all, you can't help how you feel.' He declined the return of his hanky and Mavis put it in her handbag, a tiny smile of gratitude on her face.
'I'll wash it and get it back to you,' she sniffed.
'Does that mean I can see you again?' He looked directly into her mink brown eyes and held her gaze.

VICTORY IN EUROPE

The air sizzled around Mavis. He needed to know more about her.

'I think so,' she said eventually, smiling coyly. 'That would be nice.'

-o0o-

Five weeks later, they were married in St Tarcissus Catholic Church in Camberley. It was a quiet affair; Agnes was a bridesmaid, and her brother was best man. George, Mavis's great uncle, gave her away. A few of the bride's friends attended, but no friends of Bert's appeared. He said all his true mates had already deployed and Mavis didn't think any more of it. The ceremony was conducted by Canon Twomey, the first Chaplain to the RMC, Sandhurst, who was also the first parish priest of Camberley, and who knew Mavis and her late parents well, Mavis having attended the local Catholic school and the family always attended Sunday Mass.

VICTORY IN EUROPE

Mavis wore a slate grey two piece she'd purchased from Pages Departmental Store. She'd spotted it long before meeting Bert and proved to be an inspired purchase for which she'd saved her clothing coupons. Feeling the bee's knees wearing it and her much loved navy court shoes, Mavis carried a bunch of Freesias grown in Agnes's garden. The radiant bride also wore a little blue hat with a short veil covering her eyes made especially for her by one of her neighbours who used to be a milliner in London before the war.

After the ceremony, Bert and Mavis were driven away from church by Archie Purvey, who owned the local taxi and petrol pumps, and who'd managed to save some petrol for special occasions which he was happy to use. His family lived next to Mavis when they were growing up.

The wedding guests celebrated with the happy couple at the Bull and Butcher public house in Sandhurst, who provided sandwiches and homemade scones and cake, having collected the guest's food coupons

VICTORY IN EUROPE

so they'd be able to provide a small buffet. The bar was briefly closed to non-guests, and everyone purchased their own drinks following a toast to the happy couple with Pale Sherry paid for courtesy of Bert.

A honeymoon was out of the question, so the happy couple were driven back to Mavis's home to spend their first night as Mr and Mrs Green. The house had been in her family for several generations, having been purchased with the winnings from a card game a family member had won on a Saturday night in the Wellington Arms.

An officer cadet had fallen out with some of the drinkers when he lost a bet over something long forgotten with time, and a fight ensued. It was broken up by the local Bobby, who was enjoying a quiet free pint before continuing his usual stroll around the village before the pub closed.

He suggested they find another way to heal their differences and for some daft reason the Officer Cadet agreed to a game of cards, winner takes all.

VICTORY IN EUROPE

Little did he know that Mavis's relation had once been a Mississippi steamboat gambler and, before he knew it, the Cadet had lost enough money for her relative to purchase the house she now called home, with enough for a substantial nest-egg to be put aside.

Well, that was the story Mavis was told by her dad and no-one in the village ever disputed it. Although, what an Officer Cadet was doing in a local pub was a mystery because they weren't supposed to socialise within six miles of the College and besides, the College hadn't even been there at that time. Whatever really happened remained a mystery and after a while, no-one ever talked of it again.

Inheriting her own property with a small monthly income at the age of twenty-three, following the death of both parents, had made Mavis a bit of a catch and she'd never been short of male suitors, but she'd always wanted that bit more from a husband. Meeting Bert changed all that. Suddenly she was content to be a wife and eventually, she supposed, a mother. All thoughts of travelling the world and wanting more from life vanished into thin air that night at the Agincourt. And now here she was. Married.

>Agnes was relieved. She'd feared being so choosy Mavis would be left on the shelf. Agnes, being the same age as her friend, worried about being left a spinster as well, but she was sure she'd find herself a husband at the Agincourt or die trying. In some respects, the war came as a blessing, in her opinion.

-oOo-

Bert couldn't believe his luck. Mavis was a good-looking girl, quite personable, and as soon as he'd realised she'd got property and a small income of her own, he decided he was going to marry her. After all, as her husband, what was hers would inevitably become his. He knew he had charm and could twist any girl he fancied around his little finger, and it didn't take much to sweep sweet Mavis off her feet.

VICTORY IN EUROPE

All his life, he'd longed to be someone. Orphaned so young and being put through the Duke of York School had taught him to rely on no-one but himself, to go after something and get it. However, he'd not gone through the school known as Bert Green.

That was a name he'd assumed just prior to – very reluctantly - joining the army. It was easy enough to adopt the identity of a school mate who'd invited him to spend a weekend with a maiden aunt in London prior to signing their papers of Attestation. It was sheer luck they were staying with her when her street was bombed, and she and his friend were killed. He'd been in the privy at the bottom of the garden and, apart from being unceremoniously blown off the throne, he'd escaped any injuries.

Confused momentarily and shaken - it had been a terrible shock to hear his friend being pronounced dead by a passing air-raid warden who, having laid his body and that of the aunt in the backyard, went off in search of a Policeman. An idea flashed into his head and wouldn't go. It took him moments to go through his friend's pockets, removing his Identity Card and other items which would confirm his identity. He hunted through the rubble and found a few items belonging to Bert and himself. Before the warden returned, he'd replaced Bert's ID and items with his own. From that moment on, David Balfour was dead, and he became Bert Green. He envisaged a life of freedom ahead of him, and joining the army was not part of his plans. Now David was dead. He could go anywhere, do whatever he wanted, but first he would need to find another body, a civilian's, and use their ID to completely disappear. He needed time to think, and using various identities would be a great way to do it.

Unfortunately, his good luck failed him almost straight away. The warden returned too quickly with an Army Officer who, upon seeing David, asked for his ID before he could destroy Bert's call-up papers. Following a check of the dead man's personal possessions and identity, the Officer told the frustrated young man – whose description bore a striking resemblance to his dead friend - to fall in beside him as he returned to his command nearby. David was furious, but couldn't get out of it. Bert's papers indicated he was about to sign up and the Officer took control of things from thereon. Bert signed his Attestation papers soon after and was sent to Black Down camp in Camberley, Surrey, to begin basic training.

His plans on hold, Bert decided to bide his time because he couldn't risk going absent without leave so soon. He needed to find a way out, and fast. Things were not going to plan.

Mavis had been pointed out to him a couple of times at the Agincourt before the afternoon he'd caught her eye, by which time he'd found out as much as he could about her. Mavis would be his meal ticket to a better life. Somehow, he had to get his hands on her house and subsequently her money. Marriage was a small price to pay. Bert had plans, and the war was the perfect cover for what he wanted to achieve. All he had to do was play the loving husband for a little while.

-o0o-

Bert was recalled to Black Down forty-eight hours after the wedding, the time permitted by the Army for wedding leave and he kissed his bride goodbye and he set off jauntily, happy in the belief that he would now have access to his wife's money and that he'd be added to her Will that very day when Mavis was visited by the family solicitor, Mr Rowberry of Messers Rowberry, Rowberry, and sons. The partners and sons were all quite elderly and well respected and had acted for Mavis's family since the early days of the family change in fortune.

Unknown to Bert, Mr Rowberry had reminded Mavis prior to her marriage - which he'd been obliged to do - that her Trust Fund had a safe-guard written in which precluded any future spouse having rights over or even access to her house or her money and Trust Fund. His visit was to include Bert and his in a codicil to her Will and Trust Fund.

VICTORY IN EUROPE

He'd advised her not to allow her future husband to have the full facts about her financial status. The solicitor was uneasy that Mavis knew so little about the man she was to marry and had even offered to find out more about him for her. Mavis was adamant that he did not poke his nose into her romantic affairs. Bert was everything she'd ever wanted, and that was all anyone needed to know. She wasn't too sure what her solicitor was getting at and what it all meant and whilst she agreed Mr Rowberry knew his business regarding Wills and such like, he was an old bachelor, so what did he know about love?

She agreed reluctantly to the codicil he wanted to add, which would prevent Bert getting his hands on anything if she died or they divorced, but enabling Bert to keep all properties and monies he'd accrued in his own right prior to and during their marriage. Mavis didn't want to have any claim over his money or possessions, not that he'd mentioned any, but he didn't have family and was a lowly Private in the Army, so she was sure he didn't have assets of any description. She loved Bert for himself, not any assets he might possess.

Mavis needed to have a chat to Bert about some of this once the time was right. She'd already told him she could pay for the running of the home and would cover their expenses and that he could keep his earnings to himself. She hadn't gone into detail, but said she'd been left a little housekeeping fund to cover everything, and he had not asked about it. Mr Rowberry thought it odd Bert didn't press his then fiancée on her financial situation. Mavis didn't work as such but did voluntary work in the community to aid the War effort, which was all Bert knew as far as Mavis was aware. But the fact he never asked worried the elderly solicitor.

Her Will and Trust Fund stipulated everything she owned at the time of her death – unless she'd had children who'd inherit - would pass to Great Uncle George, her mother's uncle, or his heirs if he predeceased her. Uncle George was not aware of this and Mavis had never informed him or his children of her Will. The terms of the Trust continued to ensure that everything remained in the family on her mother's side in the event Mavis died childless, according to arrangements made following the death of her father. Poor Bert, he was oblivious of the all this as he set off. Mr Rowberry arrived soon after and Mavis signed the papers he'd prepared for her, giving details of her marriage. She promised to take her marriage certificate into his offices as soon as she could, so he'd get first-hand sight of the document.

Agnes called round on her tea break from the Post Office just two minutes away, as arranged, to witness the changes. Although she didn't have a clue as to what was being changed, she was happily sworn to secrecy. She and Mavis had been great pals since they were toddlers and if Mavis wanted her to keep quiet about something, there was rightly no-one else the bride could trust more than her.

-o0o-

VICTORY IN EUROPE

Bert called Mavis every evening. He rang the call box opposite the Wellington Arms. There was a phone box in the canteen the soldiers used and the queue most evenings was long and so it always took Mavis an age to finally speak to her new husband.

'Any news about when and where you might go?' She asked every evening. 'Can you come over soon, will they give you more leave?'

'Nope, you know I've had my allotted leave, and in any case, you know how it is. I can't say anything about my deployment.'

'Yes, I know, 'loose lips sink ships,' I realise that, but it's so cruel.' Mavis sighed. 'If only there wasn't a war…'

'How did it go with the solicitor bloke?' Bert tried to sound casual.

'It was all right, just formalities, really. I told you before he had to have our wedding lines for his records and things like that. Nothing important.' She hated being so vague, but was mindful of the advice given her. 'Anyway, nothing for you to worry about. Like I told you, Bert, I have some money to pay for all the household bills and what you have is your own, so that's something, isn't it?'

'Of course, it's swell and generous of you, sweetheart, but it's all a bit over my head, I mean, a girl like you not needing to work. It's like being married to one of them nobs who live up the top of Camberley in them big houses.' He waited, wondering if she might tell him more, but the pips went, and he said he didn't have any more coins.
'Have to go darling, I'll phone tomorrow.' He managed before they got cut off.

Bert slammed the phone down on its receiver, angry he hadn't got more out of her. He was going to have to see her and soon. If he got deployed earlier than expected, all his plans would be messed up. Not that he planned on being deployed anywhere, if he had his way.

-o0o-

VICTORY IN EUROPE

The blackout observed, Mavis settled down to listen to the wireless whilst she read. She'd been to the library earlier and picked up several books to keep her occupied during the long evenings.

It never worried her being on her own before, but since Bert – everything these days went into the category of *Before and After Bert,* she mused, she'd felt lonely without him.

Unlike many of her friends, she'd not rushed into marriage as soon as she was able, often to escape the constraints of a domineering father or too many siblings to help care for. Mavis was all of twenty-five, old by the standard of the day, to be getting married.

But she'd never felt the pressure because she'd never had to worry about finances, a dominant father, or siblings to escape. She was glad she hadn't felt obliged to get hitched to the first local boy who'd asked, and several had. Mavis knew she'd been right

VICTORY IN EUROPE

to wait and now she her reward, Bert. The man of her dreams.

She was beginning to fall asleep, her book rested on her lap and the wireless became fainter and fainter, as she drifted. She awoke with a start; she felt a presence in the room. Turning her head slowly, bleary-eyed, she could make out the figure of someone sitting in her dad's chair by the fireplace. Stunned, she leaped to her feet, wondering if her father had returned from the dead.

'Take it easy, Mavis, it's me, Bert,' the figure moved towards her and she gasped with shock.

'Bert, you gave me such a fright. What are you doing here?' Nerves crackled through her body as her heart thumped. She sat down heavily, her legs wobbled and threatened to give way beneath her.

'I got a last-minute leave for the night, got to be back by five in the morning, so I decided to visit my dear wife and surprise her.' He grinned, leaned over her and kissed her long and hard on the mouth.

Mavis couldn't believe it.

VICTORY IN EUROPE

'I've made you some tea, Mavis. I thought you'd like one once you woke up.' He handed her a cup of steaming tea. 'Drink up, there's a pot made, and then we can chat.'

'Chat?' What about?' Mavis accepted the tea and blew on it before taking a sip. 'I miss my sugar,' she added pulling a face. She'd given up her sugar ration to her widowed neighbour who had six kids to feed.

'Drink up, there's a good girl,' Bert encouraged her, watching her carefully.

'You not having one, Bert?'

'Nope, had enough in the canteen earlier.' He sat down and lit a cigarette. Mavis didn't mind him smoking, but not in the house. 'You put that out Bert or go up the back garden.' She complained, 'I told you, no smoking indoors.'

'All right, keep your hair on girl,' he stubbed the cigarette out on the hearth. 'There, happy?'

'Have you eaten? I can make something if you want.'
Mavis stood up and took her cup into the scullery.
'What do you fancy?'
'Told you, been in the canteen already, don't bother.'
Bert had a quick look round the room but there wasn't any sign of any legal-looking paperwork.

'No bother darling,' Mavis returned wearing her apron. 'I can make you bacon and eggs. I've got my ration still and I can do some potatoes from the garden. There's bread and butter if you fancy. What do you say?'
Bert was not in the mood for food but had a quick rethink. If she was busy in the kitchen, he could have a better look around. There might be cash or jewellery he could have, not to mention anything else he could find worth taking and flogging.
'If it's no trouble, Mavis, that would be wonderful.' He called and added, 'I'll have a wash and then read the paper while you're busy, but first finish the tea off, waste not, want not.'

VICTORY IN EUROPE

'That's right, you make yourself at home and I can play wifey,' a delighted Mavis shouted from the kitchen, as she poured herself another cuppa. 'You go on, have a bath if you want. There's hot water enough on the range and I'll shout when I'm ready. Fill the bath from there. It's quicker than getting the boiler going.'

Mavis's indoor upstairs bathroom impressed Bert, and he enjoyed using it, but this evening he wouldn't get in the bath. He'd fill it, pretending to bathe, using the time to search Mavis's bedrooms; his first opportunity since they married.

-o0o-

His meal finished, Bert pushed his plate aside and wiped his mouth on the napkin provided. Mavis set a lovely table just like in a posh café and she was a good cook, no denying it.

'That was lovely girl, very tasty,' he licked his lips. Mavis handed him a glass of Mackeson stout. 'Nice surprise, thanks.'

VICTORY IN EUROPE

'My mum had it when she was ill, doctor said it was full of iron to build her up.' Mavis cleared the dishes and settled next to him on her sagging sofa, a cup of tea on the table beside her made by Bert.

'Mavis, you spoil me.' Her new husband kissed her forehead and Mavis felt safe, happy, and content. She snuggled closer. If only the war was over and we could settle into a life together, she thought, as Bert stroked her hair.

'That's what I want to do, spoil you and make you happy, Bert.' she smiled up at him, trusting, amazed that she'd at last found her true love.

'You make me happy too,' he lied, wondering how to bring up the topic of her nest-egg. They snuggled in silence for a few minutes before Bert said, 'that Rowberry bloke. Did he sort out everything with you?'
'Yes, I was meaning to talk to you, Bert, about how we should arrange things, you know.' She sat upright and turned to him. 'I've a little housekeeping fund. My dad left me as you know, and this house is mine, so

VICTORY IN EUROPE

you don't need to give me an allowance from your wages, Bert, it's all arranged.'

'Yes, you said something before we got married. That's nice and all that, but you should let me contribute,' he said without conviction.

'You're going away to fight, save your money for when you come back, and we can use it for something special, Bert. Really, it's not a problem.'

'If you insist sweetheart, but you should tell me just what sort of allowance you have. I'm your husband after-all and we promised not to have secrets.'

'Nothing to tell. You know what there is to know. I don't have lots of money. Like I said, if you want to save for our future whilst you're away, that would be grand.' She felt bad lying, but she respected Mr Rowberry's advice. 'Just come back to me, Bert, safe and sound.'

Bert fell silent. He'd helped himself to her cash box contents and her best jewellery, left to her by her mother, he was sure. It would fetch a bob or two. He was going to have to act fast if he was going to gain anything from this marriage.

The soldier went to bed that night, his mind full of ideas and plans on how to get his hands on all his wife's assets. Mavis slept happy in the knowledge she had a good man at her side and a rosy future once life returned to normal and peace was restored. She slept a dreamless sleep aided by the mickey-fin Bert had slipped into her final drink of the evening.

Bert left before dawn, silently wishing the unconscious Mavis goodbye. No-one saw him ride off on a bike he'd stolen from outside the railway station the previous evening. Soon he'd never have to see her again if all went to plan.

-o0o-

Mr Rowberry looked up from his paperwork in confusion to see Bert Green standing over him, a gun in his hand and menace written across his face.

'How did you get into my home?' The solicitor rose, but Bert shoved him back into his chair.

'Ways and means.' Bert waved the gun in the terrified man's face. 'Shut up and do as I say, or you'll wish you'd never been born.

An hour later Bert let himself out of the solicitor's home and got on his bike, headed back to camp. He hid the bike in the bushes at the entrance to the camp. It might come in handy again, he thought.

In his pocket he'd got a copy of his marriage certificate, and his wife's Will and Trust details which the obliging solicitor had made alterations to, setting aside the codicil Mavis had signed, and now naming Bert as her sole heir with control over her finances and assets in a new codicil. Mr Rowberry's sister lived in and often worked as his secretary.
Bert had her join them at gunpoint to type the new documents and witness his wife's signature, as Bert

forged it on the documents and copies. He'd spent many hours in his barracks, getting it just right.

He left the solicitor and his sister in their final resting place in the cellar of their shared home before heading back to camp. By the time they were discovered, he'd be long gone.

There wasn't any reason to suspect Bert of any involvement in what he'd made look like a double suicide, he'd placed the gun in the solicitor's hand and he'd worn gloves throughout and had ensured no-one had seen him enter or leave the premises.

He still had to deal with Mavis, somehow.

-o0o-

He rang Mavis as planned that evening and prayed she hadn't missed anything he'd stolen, but all she could talk about was a terrible headache she'd woken with. He persuaded her she might be threatening influenza or similar.

VICTORY IN EUROPE

He told her he'd be over to see her later that night to check on her and to say goodbye. His unit was being deployed the next day, and he wanted to see her, even if it meant sneaking off camp to do it.

Agnes couldn't console her friend when Mavis called in on her for a brief natter, following her conversation with Bert. Bert was finally going off to war and Mavis was fearful she'd never see him again. The two friends cried together before Mavis returned home, devastated at the thought of seeing her husband for the last time.

David had managed to acquire several identities since he'd stolen Bert Green's, which he knew he could fall back on if the need arose. He planned to ditch Bert's as soon as he could, doing a moonlight flit from the camp and the Army, the first opportunity he had. So far, it had served his purpose to stay in training, but now he needed to escape before he ended up in France or somewhere worse.

VICTORY IN EUROPE

First, he had to get rid of Mavis so that he could claim her estate before disappearing forever. Simple in theory but fraught with obstacles. Imminent deployment has messed up his plans, forced his hand. There was no way he was fighting anywhere, but he couldn't hang around waiting to inherit, either. Bert was fuming when Mavis said she'd told Agnes he was calling in before deployment. 'Who else did you tell about me coming this evening?' He almost shouted.

'No-one, Bert, I've been in bed most of the day with my bad head. It seems to be getting worse.' She thought he looked strange. 'Are you angry with me?' 'Of course not, now sit down and I'll make you a nice cuppa,' he offered. His plans to get rid of her were falling apart and he wondered if he could slip her one final mickey-fin and then rush over to Agnes's place to see to her too. It was all going wrong. He felt panic rising as he desperately tried to think of a way to despatch both women and not be suspected.

VICTORY IN EUROPE

'You will write when you can Bert, I'll be waiting by the letter box every day?'

'Of course, I shall never fear.'

He had a horrible feeling he'd have to find another time and method of getting rid of his wife.

He needed to be able to claim immediately and not be suspected of involvement in what he planned for her. Then he'd disappear and become someone else. There was no way he was returning to camp, and the prospect of really having taking part in the war filled him with dread and anger.

Now he wondered how his wife's suicide, her despair at his leaving to go into battle, could be explained if Agnes died as well. He wanted to smash his fists into the wall with frustration. Mavis watched his agitation with mounting unhappiness, mistakenly thinking her husband was as terrified of leaving her as she was of letting him go.

A loud bang on the front door shook him from his revelry, and Mavis nearly jumped out of her skin. 'I

thought you said no-one else was popping in this evening,' he hissed at her, frustrated at the intrusion.
'I'll get rid of whoever it is,' Mavis said, and closed the sitting room door behind her as she went into the hall.
'Mrs Green?' Two large Military Policemen stood on her doorstep.
'Yes, can I help you?' Her heart sank as she looked from one to the other.
'Is your husband with you this evening, Private Bert Green?' One of them asked, removing his hat.
'Yes, he is. Shall I fetch him?' Mavis licked her lips nervously.
'No need misses. We'll fetch him ourselves. Lead the way.' The shorter, stockier man said.

Before Mavis could reply, the two men entered the hall and headed for the sitting room. Bert shouted, and there was a struggle before they frog-marched him out of the front door. 'Bert, Bert, what' happening?'

VICTORY IN EUROPE

'He's absent without leave misses, he's not going anywhere again unless it's on a ship. The Army has plans for your husband. He's under arrest.'
'Mavis, Mavis,' shouted Bert as they bundled him into the jeep waiting outside on the road.

Mavis ran out and grabbed the MP nearest. 'we can't say goodbye like this, we've only just got married. Let me kiss him goodbye, please.'
'Quick then, we have others to round up.'
'I love you Bert, take care and keep safe. We'll meet again soon; I know we will.' Mavis sobbed as Bert planted a kiss on her tear drenched lips.
'Bye Mavis, wait for me, I'll be back,' he shouted wondering how and when he'd get his hands on her money. 'Keep safe,' he added. I need you to live through this bloody war, he muttered to himself as they drove him into the night.

-o0o-

VICTORY IN EUROPE

Letters for Mavis arrived now and again, heavily censored, but full of how he missed and loved her. Bert wasn't stupid. He wanted to keep the fire alight whilst he was away, and her letters back reassured him she was well and still loved him.

He'd find a route back to her money one way or another unless a better prospect came his way, and he was always looking for opportunities. In fact, there was an Italian countess whose husband had died helping the British shortly after he'd arrived in France.

She was a prospect, but he wasn't giving up on Mavis just yet. The war must end soon, surely.

Mavis wrote to him about the disappearance of Mr Rowberry and his sister and how, eventually, they'd been found dead in their cellar, and it appeared to be some sort of double suicide, poor souls. They never harmed anyone, and the reason was a mystery.

Bert wrote back, expressing his horror and sympathies. He wrote of his complete amazement when she said some of her jewellery and cash had vanished. She didn't know when they'd gone, but Agnes said she'd seen some Gypsies in the village not long after Bert had been arrested by the MPs, and everyone thought they'd got into the house at some point. The police thought it odd that was all they'd taken, but the Gypsies had long gone by then and there was nothing to be done. Bert smirked; he'd eventually got a pretty penny for her things.

He had to find a way to get out of France and back to her money. It was not part of his plan, being shot at by the Germans. He tried hard to find a way to escape, to find another identity, but easier planned than done. There was no way he'd pass as a Frenchman to get out of France.

Three years passed, and suddenly the letters stopped. Mavis was beside herself with worry and grief. No-one could tell her anything about her husband's fate, of course, and so she waited. And then the telegram arrived. But still she waited. She was sure he was alive somewhere.

VICTORY IN EUROPE

The War ended, just like that. She couldn't believe it. Men were coming home, but so far her Bert hadn't managed to return. Mavis refused to believe the telegram, until they showed her his body. She would go on waiting and hoping.

VE Day arrived and everyone celebrated. She even joined in. But although Mavis felt relief that the fighting was over, she still felt deep down that Bert was still alive somewhere and that somehow, one day, they'd meet again.

In her chateau in France once more, the Italian Countess stood in front of her late husband's safe in complete disbelief. It was empty. She ran from room to room and then into the vast grounds which had once again been returned to her following the occupation, and screamed her lover's name over and over again, but to no avail. He had gone. Richard had gone and so had all her money and jewellery, and she wondered if they'd ever meet again.

VICTORY IN EUROPE

No longer David, Bert, or Richard, Oscar Manning managed to find his way to America courtesy of a dead G.I, thanks to the confusion following the end of the war. He had plenty of money and the jewellery he'd stolen from his Italian fiancée would fetch a tidy sum, he was sure. He was about to start a new life, a new world was there for the taking and as far as he was concerned, he'd never meet any of his fiancées ever again.

… VICTORY IN EUROPE …

99TH SQUADRON

By Audrina Lane

2020

Holding his hand, I listened to the beep of the machine. I knew he didn't have long to go, but 99 years old and 12 days into his 100th year was quite an achievement for my grandad. As he drifted off to sleep, I felt my own eyelids dropping, but I didn't want to waste any last moments with him. I slipped away into the kitchen and put the kettle on.

On my way back through to the bedroom, I paused by the bookshelf and reached for the well-worn, leather

VICTORY IN EUROPE

bound photo album. It was the one with all his Royal Air Force pictures in and memories of the war.

Taking the comfy chair next to him, I opened the first page and gazed at a young man in uniform that I had never known. He looked so proud as he stared into the lens. The photo sepia and the edges are well worn. The next page held various squadron photos until recently he'd still been able to name them all. He told me of Lofthouse, who was the prankster of the bunch and always getting into scrapes.

Then there was Wilding, who was serious and sadly the first lost in a bombing raid. I turned the page again and stared at the patterned patchwork fields, a shot taken from the inside of the plane. I shut my eyes, remembering the first time I had really asked my Gramps about the war and he'd shown me the picture.

I heard his voice echoing in my head, "Look closer Clare, it's not just fields taken from a plane."

VICTORY IN EUROPE

I had, and that was when I spotted the bomb, suspended in the centre on its descent onto a landscape that was clearly not England. A cold chill had reached fingers across the nape of my neck. They still did it now as I wondered where had been the destination for the bomb? A military base, the front line or a mis-timed release that could have landed on anywhere or anyone? He had never told me that. I guess I would never know.

Closing my eyes for a moment, I reached to link my fingers with his old ones. He had spent all his life working on machines. He had not been the glory of a fighter pilot, not a magnificent man in his flying machine.

Instead, he was the ground crew, making sure that the planes were serviced or repaired in time for the next sortie across the channel. Then he'd been moved out of Britain and became part of the Pacific attack, stationed in India and the Coco Islands.

VICTORY IN EUROPE

Suddenly the machine started to beep a little faster, and I turned to see that his eyes were open, and his grip had tightened.

"What are you doing?"

"Just remembering you telling me about the war and showing me these photos," I said.

"Ah, bless. They were some of the best days and some of the worst." He coughed out the last word and I passed him the glass of water so he could take a sip through the straw. He closed his eyes once more and, as he went to sleep, I followed him into his dream, an imposter in the shadows.

1945

The sun was beating down on my face, the heat reflecting up from the light sand of the beach. The bombing raids on England had been devastating at times, with the coastline and the major cities of

VICTORY IN EUROPE

London, Birmingham and Coventry also facing a daily and nightly barrage.

I wondered if we would win this fight, as I twisted the spanner and tightened the bolts that had shaken loose on the fuselage. The pilot was lounging in the shade, what little there was on the beach. The conditions were vastly different, with the main part of our work taking place early in the morning or later in the evening.

This was the furthest I had ever been from home, and I often thought about my life back there. Ena, the girl I had met back in the early days when I'd first signed up. We had been married and I knew that when or if I returned, my legacy was assured. My wife had been pregnant when I'd flown away to what had seemed to me to be the other end of the world.

America had finally joined the war in full force after Japan had hit them hard at Pearl Harbour. I had been sent from India to the Coco Islands to provide

VICTORY IN EUROPE

bombing raids from the small airfield against Japan. It was strange to know that I was so far away from home, yet crucial to the war effort.

The Liberator bombers were what I worked on as they were able to provide long range bombing raids. The heat from the metal on the plane was intense, but I was determined to get the job finished and let the pilot get back in the air.

When I wasn't working, I was chatting, doing my clothes, washing in the sea water and generally trying to keep cool. I lived in shorts and very little else, as the high humidity just made me sweat and feel uncomfortable all the time. It was such a contrast to life in England and I somehow knew that I'd probably never come back to this part of the world again.

The most dangerous part of life on the island was sleeping. Our tents were pitched beneath the coconut trees and they would just fall when they were ready, sometimes bringing down the tree branches as well. I

VICTORY IN EUROPE

had a few lucky escapes. All the troops used to joke that being killed by a falling coconut would not warrant a medal or military honours.

We had a radio to keep in touch with the news and as the 8th May, 1945 dawned nothing felt any different until we all heard a shout from the NAAFI and we scrambled from our places on the sand or in the sea to find out what was happening and whether it was good news of bad. It was good; the war was over in Europe with Hitler and Germany surrendering to the Allied forces.

But would it be the same for us, forgotten in the Pacific Ocean? We raised a quick glass to our boys on the Western front, but then it was back to work. More screws and bolts to check and tighten before the next flight sortie took off. Then it was the long wait until they returned.

I always found that part the hardest, waiting to hear the drone of the Liberator engines returning to base.

VICTORY IN EUROPE

As chance would have it, our bombing raids were very few as the atomic bomb was dropped on Japan and that was the beginning of the end of the Pacific war.

I had been in the RAF since the start of the war, so I was lucky enough to be one of the first men to start the journey home. I remembered the buzz of the plane engines as we took off. We actually had to stand until the plane was in flight and it was one of the memories I always came back to in the years since. Through the chink in the bomb doors I watched the landing strip fall away before a view of the small island, surrounded by the bright blue of the Pacific ocean. We had been such a small part of a huge operation, with so many lives lost along the way.

I was home, in time for Christmas Day in 1945, my beautiful wife waiting for me as I stepped through the front door. I never had to explain what I had lived through.

When she looked into my eyes, all I saw was her love and relief that I was back in her arms and that our daughter Sandra would not grow up with only one parent. We were a family, we had survived, we were victorious.

2020

I closed the photo album as my grandad's hand seemed to tighten its grip over mine.
"I see her," he whispered.
"Who, who do you see?" I replied, shaken that he had found some words again.
"My Ena, she waited for me to return to her and now it is time. My war is over."
A tear slid slowly down his cheek, following the wrinkles of age and time.
"It was over years ago. You lived an amazing…." I never finished my sentence. I heard him take a deep sighing breath before he passed away. I laid my head

VICTORY IN EUROPE

on his hand, feeling the warmth slip away from his skin. He had been and would always be my hero.

Dedicated to Alfred Lane, my gramps.

VICTORY IN EUROPE

THE AUTHORS

Karen J Mossman

Paul White

https://bit.ly/paulswebsite

Claire Plaisted

Julia Blake

http://juliablakeauthor.co.uk/books/

Jane Risdon

https://janerisdon.com/books/

Audrina Lane

https://www.audrinalane.co.uk/

About Electric Eclectic Books

Electric Eclectic Books was founded in 2017 by Paul White, who had a simple idea: to help authors publish introductory novellas, giving readers a taste of 'new to you' authors' works.

While the publishing of new titles under the brand ended in 2024, the existing collection remains a great way to discover these 'new-to-you' authors and explore different styles and genres.

Who knows what the future holds? We might just bring Electric Eclectic back to life someday.

For now, happy reading.

VICTORY IN EUROPE

OTHER ELECTRIC ECLECTIC ANTHOLOGIES

Mothballs

Butterfly Bats

Mayfly Recitals

Printed in Great Britain
by Amazon